Samantha: For Levi, Holden, and Penelope. Thank you for leaving a little less order and a lot more joy in my world with each passing day.

Tacey: To William Jr., William III, Anderson, and Hunter. May you choose every day to make the world a little more new. May you always smile and always be you. I love you so very much!

Charitable Partnership with U.S. Soccer Foundation

A portion of the proceeds from the sale of this book will go to the U.S. Soccer Foundation. The mission of the U.S. Soccer Foundation is to provide underserved communities access to innovative play spaces and evidence-based soccer programs that instill hope, foster well-being, and help youth achieve their fullest potential.

Samantha and Tacey's lives have been uniquely touched by the sport of soccer. Samantha grew up playing competitively and played at Tulane University (go Green Wave!). In 2005, when Hurricane Katrina hit, she evacuated New Orleans alongside her soccer team and learned countless lessons in hope, resilience, and personal growth. In addition, Samantha's husband, Sam Cronin, and Tacey's husband, William Hesmer, both played collegiately at Wake Forest University and professionally in Major League Soccer. Their time at Wake Forest and in the MLS produced life-long friendships and priceless memories. These days, in full-circle fashion, Samantha and Tacey (and their dear husbands) can be found behind the car pool wheel shuttling their kids back and forth to soccer practices of their own.

At its core, *Leave a Little More* celebrates the fact that our daily activities can be powerful opportunities to leave the world a better place. Samantha and Tacey have witnessed firsthand how deeply this theme resonates with the lessons that can be learned through soccer. They are thrilled to be giving back to the sport that has played such a powerful role in the lives of so many. For more information on the U.S. Soccer Foundation, please visit ussoccerfoundation.org., or follow them on Twitter at @ussoccerfndn and Instagram at @ussoccerfoundation.

www.mascotbooks.com

Leave a Little More

For more information, please contact
Mascot Kids, an imprint of Amplify Publishing Group
620 Herndon Parkway #320
Herndon, VA 20170
info@mascotbooks.com

Library of Congress Control Number: 2022907358

CPSIA Code: PRT0522A
ISBN-13: 978-1-63755-525-5

Printed in the United States

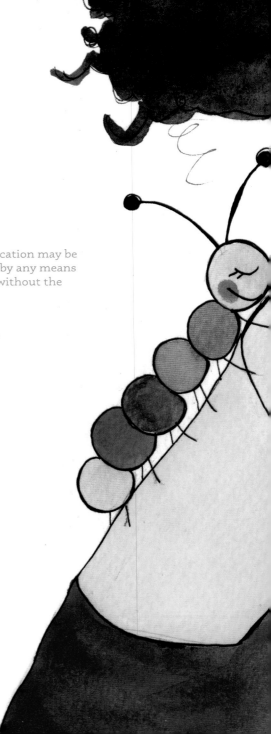

Leave a Little More

Samantha Cronin
Illustrated by Tacey Hesmer

Today is a new day! It matters. But why?
Today can be more than just time ticking by.

Today you can change. You can build on before.
Today you can choose to leave a little more.

You can choose to paint . . .
leave a little more art.

Or choose to read books . . .
leave a little more heart.

You can choose to dance . . .
leave a little more flare.

Or choose to fly high . . .
leave a little more air.

You can choose to race . . .
leave a little more glee.

Or choose to splish-splash . . .
leave a little more free.

You can choose to sow . . .
leave a little more green.

Or choose to pick up . . .
leave a little more clean.

You can choose to teach . . .
leave a little more skill.

Or choose to observe . . .
leave a little more still.

You can choose to seek . . .
leave a little more found.

Or choose to speak out . . .
leave a little more sound.

You can choose to serve . . .
leave a little more care.

Or choose to take turns . . .
leave a little more fair.

You can choose to smile . . .
leave a little more cheer.

Or choose to give hugs . . .
leave a little more dear.

Yes, today you are wild and you're free and you're you . . .

and you're making a difference in *all* that you do.

Every day is a chance—

every choice is one too . . .

Discussion Guide

At the beginning of the book, the space between the children's houses is wide open—a blank slate of white space. But by the end, it is overflowing with rich, colorful memories and vibrant details reflecting the day they spent together. In a way, that's how the world works—every day is a fresh start, a blank page. Throughout our day, we make a series of seemingly ordinary choices. But it's those very ordinary choices that gradually fill our page, our world, with something extraordinary that wasn't there before.

Here are a few questions and ideas to keep the conversation going with the people in your life:

1. If you look closely at the last page, can you find something from every activity the two friends did throughout their day? You may need to flip back through the book!

2. Even the inchworm's actions matter. Can you find him on every page?

3. How might the last page look different if the friends had made different choices throughout their day?

4. What are some things you chose to do today? How did those choices impact the world around you? (Hint: Try filling in the blanks: Today I chose to _____, which left a little more _____ in the world.)

5. Can you think of anything that someone else did today that made your day better? (Hint: Try filling in the blanks: Today _____ chose to _____, which left my world a little more _____.)

6. Find a blank sheet of paper. What does it look like? Now gather some art supplies and decorate the paper to show some of the activities or actions you chose to do today. Paint, draw, cut and paste—get creative! How does the paper look when you're done? What's different from before?

7. Get a notebook and start keeping a "Leave a Little More" journal. At the end of every day, jot down one thing you (or somebody else) did that day, and how it left the world a little different, a little changed, a little better than before.

8. Parents/Teachers/Coaches: Next time you're sitting around the dinner table, gathered at circle time, or chatting with your players, ask everyone to share a choice they made that day and how it impacted somebody or something around them. It's a fun way to connect and hear about each other's days, while reinforcing the truth that the little things your kids (and you!) do each day are, in fact, big things.

About the Author

Samantha Cronin is a former Google-employee-turned-writer, mama bear to three delightfully wild hooligans, and proud wife to a man she loves very much, whose name is also Sam. She currently works as the contracts and royalties manager at Nelson Literary Agency and is a member of the Society of Children's Book Writers and Illustrators. When she's not working, writing, or wrangling tiny humans, she's busy believing in the power of everyday moments (and strong coffee). Come say hello on Twitter or Instagram.

⬡ @ladysamcronin
🐦 @ladysamcronin

About the Illustrator

Tacey Hesmer is a Raleigh-based artist, boy mom of three, and doggie mom of one. She began her artistic journey studying acting in New York and Los Angeles. By day, she pours her soul into abstract expressionism paintings for her original art company (visit tacey.co for more info) and spreads love on her family every chance she gets. By night, she dreams of whimsical illustrations and laundry that folds itself. She is also the illustrator of *Dinosaurs Love Donuts* (2019). You can find her on Instagram, and when she's feeling especially hip, TikTok.

@tacey.co

@taceyhesmer